I0750326

H. G. Wells

A Dream of Armageddon

Fantastica

LONDON · NEW YORK · TORONTO · SAO PAULO · MOSCOW
PARIS · MADRID · BERLIN · ROME · MEXICO CITY · MUMBAI · SEOUL · DOHA
TOKYO · SYDNEY · CAPE TOWN · AUCKLAND · BEIJING

New Edition

Published by Fantastica
www.imediaworld.uk

This Edition first published in 2018

ISBN: 9781787245808

CONTENTS

A DREAM OF ARMAGEDDON

The man with the white face entered the carriage at Rugby. He moved slowly in spite of the urgency of his porter, and even while he was still on the platform I noted how ill he seemed. He dropped into the corner over against me with a sigh, made an incomplete attempt to arrange his travelling shawl, and became motionless, with his eyes staring vacantly. Presently he was moved by a sense of my observation, looked up at me, and put out a spiritless hand for his newspaper. Then he glanced again in my direction.

I feigned to read. I feared I had unwittingly embarrassed him, and in a moment I was surprised to find him speaking.

"I beg your pardon?" said I.

"That book," he repeated, pointing a lean finger, "is about dreams."

"Obviously," I answered, for it was Fortnum Roscoe's Dream States, and the title was on the cover.

He hung silent for a space as if he sought words. "Yes," he said at last, "but they tell you nothing."

I did not catch his meaning for a second.

"They don't know," he added.

I looked a little more attentively at his face.

"There are dreams," he said, "and dreams."

That sort of proposition I never dispute.

"I suppose—" he hesitated. "Do you ever dream? I mean

vividly."

"I dream very little," I answered. "I doubt if I have three vivid dreams in a year."

"Ah!" he said, and seemed for a moment to collect his thoughts.

"Your dreams don't mix with your memories?" he asked abruptly.

"You don't find yourself in doubt; did this happen or did it not?"

"Hardly ever. Except just for a momentary hesitation now and then. I suppose few people do."

"Does he say—?" He indicated the book.

"Says it happens at times and gives the usual explanation about intensity of impression and the like to account for its not happening as a rule. I suppose you know something of these theories—"

"Very little—except that they are wrong."

His emaciated hand played with the strap of the window for a time. I prepared to resume reading, and that seemed to precipitate his next remark. He leant forward almost as though he would touch me.

"Isn't there something called consecutive dreaming—that goes on night after night?"

"I believe there is. There are cases given in most books on mental trouble."

"Mental trouble! Yes. I daresay there are. It's the right place for them. But what I mean—" He looked at his bony knuckles. "Is that sort of thing always dreaming? Is it dreaming? Or is it something else? Mightn't it be something else?"

I should have snubbed his persistent conversation but for the drawn anxiety of his face. I remember now the look of his faded eyes and the lids red stained—perhaps you know that look.

"I'm not just arguing about a matter of opinion," he said. "The thing's killing me."
"Dreams?"

"If you call them dreams. Night after night. Vivid!—so vivid . . . . this—" (he indicated the landscape that went streaming by the window) "seems unreal in comparison! I can scarcely remember who I am, what business I am on . . . ."

He paused. "Even now—"

"The dream is always the same—do you mean?" I asked.

"It's over."

"You mean?"

"I died."

"Died?"

"Smashed and killed, and now, so much of me as that dream was, is dead. Dead forever. I dreamt I was another man, you know, living in a different part of the world and in a different time. I dreamt that night after night. Night after night I woke into that other life. Fresh scenes and fresh happenings—until I came upon the last—"

"When you died?"

"When I died."

"And since then—"

"No," he said. "Thank God! That was the end of the dream . . ."

It was clear I was in for this dream. And after all, I had an hour before me, the light was fading fast, and Fortnum Roscoe has a dreary way with him. "Living in a different time," I said: "do you mean in some different age?"

"Yes."

"Past?"

"No, to come—to come."

"The year three thousand, for example?"

"I don't know what year it was. I did when I was asleep, when I was dreaming, that is, but not now—not now that I am awake. There's a lot of things I have forgotten since I woke out of these dreams, though I knew them at the time when I was—I suppose it was dreaming. They called the year differently from our way of calling the year . . . What did they call it?" He put his hand to his forehead. "No," said he, "I forget."

He sat smiling weakly. For a moment I feared he did not mean to tell me his dream. As a rule I hate people who tell their dreams, but this struck me differently. I proffered assistance even. "It began—" I suggested.

"It was vivid from the first. I seemed to wake up in it suddenly. And it's curious that in these dreams I am speaking of I never remembered this life I am living now. It seemed as if the dream life was enough while it lasted. Perhaps—But I will tell you how I find myself when I do my best to recall it all. I don't remember anything clearly until I found myself sitting in a sort of loggia looking out over the sea. I had been dozing, and suddenly I woke up—fresh and vivid—not a bit dreamlike—because the girl had stopped fanning me."

"The girl?"

"Yes, the girl. You must not interrupt or you will put me out."

He stopped abruptly. "You won't think I'm mad?" he said.

"No," I answered. "You've been dreaming. Tell me your dream."

"I woke up, I say, because the girl had stopped fanning me. I was not surprised to find myself there or anything of that sort, you understand. I did not feel I had fallen into it suddenly. I simply took it up at that point. Whatever memory I had of this life, this nineteenth-century life, faded as I woke, vanished like a dream. I knew all about myself, knew that my name was no longer Cooper but Hedon, and all about my position in the world. I've forgotten a lot since I woke—there's a want of connection—but it was all quite clear and matter of fact then."

He hesitated again, gripping the window strap, putting his face forward and looking up to me appealingly.

"This seems bosh to you?"

"No, no!" I cried. "Go on. Tell me what this loggia was like!"

"It was not really a loggia—I don't know what to call it. It faced south. It was small. It was all in shadow except the semicircle above the balcony that showed the sky and sea and the corner where the girl stood. I was on a couch—it was a metal couch with light striped cushions—and the girl was leaning over the balcony with her back to me. The light of the sunrise fell on her ear and cheek. Her pretty white neck and the little curls that nestled there, and her white shoulder were in the sun, and all the grace of her body was in the cool blue shadow. She was dressed—how can I describe it? It was easy and flowing. And altogether there she stood, so that it came to me how beautiful and desirable she was, as though I had never seen her before. And when at last I sighed and raised myself upon my arm she turned her face to me—"

He stopped.

"I have lived three-and-fifty years in this world. I have had mother, sisters, friends, wife and daughters—all their faces, the play of their faces, I know. But the face of this girl—it is much more real to me. I can bring it back into memory so that I see it again—I could draw it or paint it. And after all—"

He stopped—but I said nothing.

"The face of a dream—the face of a dream. She was beautiful. Not that beauty which is terrible, cold, and worshipful, like the beauty of a saint; nor that beauty that stirs fierce passions; but a sort of radiation, sweet lips that softened into smiles, and grave gray eyes. And she moved gracefully, she seemed to have part with all pleasant and gracious things—"

He stopped, and his face was downcast and hidden. Then he looked up at me and went on, making no further attempt to disguise his absolute belief in the reality of his story.

"You see, I had thrown up my plans and ambitions, thrown up all I had ever worked for or desired for her sake. I had been a master man away there in the north, with influence and property and a great reputation, but none of it had seemed worth having beside her. I had come to the place, this city of sunny pleasures with her, and left all those things to wreck and ruin just to save a remnant at least of my life. While I had been in love with her before I knew that she had any care for me, before I had imagined that she would dare—that we should dare, all my life had seemed vain and hollow, dust and ashes. It was dust and ashes. Night after night and through the long days I had longed and desired—my soul had beaten against the thing forbidden!

"But it is impossible for one man to tell another just these things. It's emotion, it's a tint, a light that comes and goes. Only while it's there, everything changes, everything. The thing is I came away and left them in their Crisis to do what they could."

"Left whom?" I asked, puzzled.

"The people up in the north there. You see—in this dream,

anyhow—I had been a big man, the sort of man men come to trust in, to group themselves about. Millions of men who had never seen me were ready to do things and risk things because of their confidence in me. I had been playing that game for years, that big laborious game, that vague, monstrous political game amidst intrigues and betrayals, speech and agitation. It was a vast weltering world, and at last I had a sort of leadership against the Gang—you know it was called the Gang—a sort of compromise of scoundrelly projects and base ambitions and vast public emotional stupidities and catch-words—the Gang that kept the world noisy and blind year by year, and all the while that it was drifting, drifting towards infinite disaster. But I can't expect you to understand the shades and complications of the year—the year something or other ahead. I had it all—down to the smallest details—in my dream. I suppose I had been dreaming of it before I awoke, and the fading outline of some queer new development I had imagined still hung about me as I rubbed my eyes. It was some grubby affair that made me thank God for the sunlight. I sat up on the couch and remained looking at the woman and rejoicing—rejoicing that I had come away out of all that tumult and folly and violence before it was too late. After all, I thought, this is life—love and beauty, desire and delight, are they not worth all those dismal struggles for vague, gigantic ends? And I blamed myself for having ever sought to be a leader when I might have given my days to love. But then, thought I, if I had not spent my early days sternly and austerely, I might have wasted myself upon vain and worthless women, and at the thought all my being went out in love and tenderness to my dear mistress, my dear lady, who had come at last and compelled me—compelled me by her invincible charm for me—to lay that life aside.

"'You are worth it,' I said, speaking without intending her to hear; 'you are worth it, my dearest one; worth pride and praise and all things. Love! to have you is worth them all together." And at the murmur of my voice she turned about.

"'Come and see,' she cried—I can hear her now—'come and see the sunrise upon Monte Solaro.'

"I remember how I sprang to my feet and joined her at the

balcony. She put a white hand upon my shoulder and pointed towards great masses of limestone, flushing, as it were, into life. I looked. But first I noted the sunlight on her face caressing the lines of her cheeks and neck. How can I describe to you the scene we had before us? We were at Capri—"

"I have been there," I said. "I have clambered up Monte Solaro and drunk vero Capri—muddy stuff like cider—at the summit."

"Ah!" said the man with the white face; "then perhaps you can tell me—you will know if this is indeed Capri. For in this life I have never been there. Let me describe it. We were in a little room, one of a vast multitude of little rooms, very cool and sunny, hollowed out of the limestone of a sort of cape, very high above the sea. The whole island, you know, was one enormous hotel, complex beyond explaining, and on the other side there were miles of floating hotels, and huge floating stages to which the flying machines came. They called it a pleasure city. Of course, there was none of that in your time—rather, I should say, is none of that now. Of course. Now!—yes.

"Well, this room of ours was at the extremity of the cape, so that one could see east and west. Eastward was a great cliff—a thousand feet high perhaps—coldly gray except for one bright edge of gold, and beyond it the Isle of the Sirens, and a falling coast that faded and passed into the hot sunrise. And when one turned to the west, distinct and near was a little bay, a little beach still in shadow. And out of that shadow rose Solaro straight and tall, flushed and golden crested, like a beauty throned, and the white moon was floating behind her in the sky. And before us from east to west stretched the many-tinted sea all dotted with little sailing boats.

"To the eastward, of course, these little boats were gray and very minute and clear, but to the westward they were little boats of gold—shining gold—almost like little flames. And just below us was a rock with an arch worn through it. The blue sea-water broke to green and foam all round the rock, and a galley came gliding out of the arch."

"I know that rock." I said. "I was nearly drowned there. It is called the Faraglioni."

"I Faraglioni? Yes, she called it that," answered the man with the white face. "There was some story—but that—"

He put his hand to his forehead again. "No," he said, "I forget that story."

"Well, that is the first thing I remember, the first dream I had, that little shaded room and the beautiful air and sky and that dear lady of mine, with her shining arms and her graceful robe, and how we sat and talked in half whispers to one another. We talked in whispers not because there was any one to hear, but because there was still such a freshness of mind between us that our thoughts were a little frightened, I think, to find themselves at last in words. And so they went softly.

"Presently we were hungry and we went from our apartment, going by a strange passage with a moving floor, until we came to the great breakfast room—there was a fountain and music. A pleasant and joyful place it was, with its sunlight and splashing, and the murmur of plucked strings. And we sat and ate and smiled at one another, and I would not heed a man who was watching me from a table near by.

"And afterwards we went on to the dancing-hall. But I cannot describe that hall. The place was enormous—larger than any building you have ever seen—and in one place there was the old gate of Capri, caught into the wall of a gallery high overhead. Light girders, stems and threads of gold, burst from the pillars like fountains, streamed like an Aurora across the roof and interlaced, like—like conjuring tricks. All about the great circle for the dancers there were beautiful figures, strange dragons, and intricate and wonderful grotesques bearing lights. The place was inundated with artificial light that shamed the newborn day. And as we went through the throng the people turned about and looked at us, for all through the world my name and face were known, and how I had suddenly thrown up pride and struggle to come to this place. And they looked also at the lady beside me, though half the story of how at last she had come to me was unknown or mistold. And few of the men who were there, I know, but judged me a happy man, in spite of all the shame and dishonour that had come upon my name.

"The air was full of music, full of harmonious scents, full of the rhythm of beautiful motions. Thousands of beautiful people swarmed about the hall, crowded the galleries, sat in a myriad recesses; they were dressed in splendid colours and crowned with flowers; thousands danced about the great circle beneath the white images of the ancient gods, and glorious processions of youths and maidens came and went. We two danced, not the dreary monotonies of your days—of this time, I mean—but dances that were beautiful, intoxicating. And even now I can see my lady dancing—dancing joyously. She danced, you know, with a serious face; she danced with a serious dignity, and yet she was smiling at me and caressing me—smiling and caressing with her eyes.

"The music was different," he murmured. "It went—I cannot describe it; but it was infinitely richer and more varied than any music that has ever come to me awake.

"And then—it was when we had done dancing—a man came to speak to me. He was a lean, resolute man, very soberly clad for that place, and already I had marked his face watching me in the breakfasting hall, and afterwards as we went along the passage I had avoided his eye. But now, as we sat in a little alcove, smiling at the pleasure of all the people who went to and fro across the shining floor, he came and touched me, and spoke to me so that I was forced to listen. And he asked that he might speak to me for a little time apart.

"'No,' I said. 'I have no secrets from this lady. What do you want to tell me?'

"He said it was a trivial matter, or at least a dry matter, for a lady to hear.

"'Perhaps for me to hear,' said I.

"He glanced at her, as though almost he would appeal to her. Then he asked me suddenly if I had heard of a great and avenging declaration that Evesham had made? Now, Evesham had always before been the man next to myself in the leadership of that great party in the north. He was a forcible, hard, and tactless man, and only I had been able to control and soften him. It was on his account even more than my own, I think, that the others had been so dismayed at my retreat. So this question about what he had done reawakened my old interest in the life I had put aside just for a moment.

"'I have taken no heed of any news for many days,' I said. 'What has Evesham been saying?'

"And with that the man began, nothing loth, and I must confess even I was struck by Evesham's reckless folly in the wild and threatening words he had used. And this messenger they had sent to me not only told me of Evesham's speech, but went on to ask counsel and to point out what need they had of me. While he talked, my lady sat a little forward and watched his face and mine.

"My old habits of scheming and organising reasserted themselves. I could even see myself suddenly returning to the north, and all the dramatic effect of it. All that this man said witnessed to the disorder of the party indeed, but not to its damage. I should go back stronger than I had come. And then I thought of my lady. You see—how can I tell you? There were certain peculiarities of our relationship—as things are I need not tell you about that—which would render her presence with me impossible. I should have had to leave her; indeed, I should have had to renounce her clearly and openly, if I was to do all that I could do in the north. And the man knew that, even as he talked to her and me, knew it as well as she did, that my steps to duty were—first, separation, then abandonment. At the touch of that thought my dream of a return was shattered. I turned on the man suddenly, as he was imagining his eloquence was gaining ground with me.

"'What have I to do with these things now?' I said. 'I have done with them. Do you think I am coquetting with your people in coming here?'

"'No,' he said. 'But—'

"'Why cannot you leave me alone. I have done with these things. I have ceased to be anything but a private man.'

"'Yes,' he answered. 'But have you thought?—this talk of war, these reckless challenges, these wild aggressions—'

"I stood up.

"'No,' I cried. 'I won't hear you. I took count of all those things, I weighed them—and I have come away.'

"He seemed to consider the possibility of persistence. He looked from me to where the lady sat regarding us.

"'War,' he said, as if he were speaking to himself, and then turned slowly from me and walked away.

"I stood, caught in the whirl of thoughts his appeal had set going.

"I heard my lady's voice.

"'Dear,' she said; 'but if they had need of you—'

"She did not finish her sentence, she let it rest there. I turned to her sweet face, and the balance of my mood swayed and reeled.

"'They want me only to do the thing they dare not do themselves,' I said. 'If they distrust Evesham they must settle with him themselves.'

"She looked at me doubtfully.

"'But war—' she said.

"I saw a doubt on her face that I had seen before, a doubt of herself and me, the first shadow of the discovery that, seen strongly and completely, must drive us apart for ever.

"Now, I was an older mind than hers, and I could sway her to this belief or that.

"'My dear one,' I said, 'you must not trouble over these things. There will be no war. Certainly there will be no war. The age of wars is past. Trust me to know the justice of this case. They have no right upon me, dearest, and no one has a right upon me. I have been free to choose my life, and I have chosen this.'

"'But war—,' she said.

"I sat down beside her. I put an arm behind her and took her hand in mine. I set myself to drive that doubt away—I set myself to fill her mind with pleasant things again. I lied to her, and in lying to her I lied also to myself. And she was only too ready to believe me, only too ready to forget.

"Very soon the shadow had gone again, and we were hastening to our bathing-place in the Grotta del Bovo Marino, where it was our custom to bathe every day. We swam and splashed one another, and in that buoyant water I seemed to become something lighter and stronger than a man. And at last we came out dripping and rejoicing and raced among the rocks. And then I put on a dry bathing-dress, and we sat to bask in the sun, and presently I nodded, resting my head against her knee, and she put her hand upon my hair and stroked it softly and I dozed. And behold! as it were with the snapping of the string of a violin, I was awakening, and I was in my own bed in Liverpool, in the life of to-day.

"Only for a time I could not believe that all these vivid moments had been no more than the substance of a dream.

"In truth, I could not believe it a dream for all the sobering reality of things about me. I bathed and dressed as it were by habit, and as I shaved I argued why I of all men should leave the woman I loved to go back to fantastic politics in the hard and strenuous north. Even if Evesham did force the world back to war, what was that to me? I was a man with the heart of a man, and why should I feel the responsibility of a deity for the way the world might go?

"You know that is not quite the way I think about affairs, about my real affairs. I am a solicitor, you know, with a point of view.

"The vision was so real, you must understand, so utterly unlike a dream that I kept perpetually recalling little irrelevant details; even the ornament of the book-cover that lay on my wife's sewing-machine in the breakfast-room recalled with the utmost vividness the gilt line that ran about the seat in the alcove where I had talked with the messenger from my deserted party. Have you ever heard of a dream that had a quality like that?"

"Like—?"

"So that afterwards you remembered little details you had forgotten."

I thought. I had never noticed the point before, but he was right.

"Never," I said. "That is what you never seem to do with dreams."

"No," he answered. "But that is just what I did. I am a solicitor, you must understand, in Liverpool, and I could not help wondering what the clients and business people I found myself talking to in my office would think if I told them suddenly I was in love with a girl who would be born a couple of hundred years or so hence, and worried about the politics of my great-great-great-grandchildren. I was chiefly busy that day negotiating a ninety-nine-year building lease. It was a private builder in a hurry, and we wanted to tie him in every possible way. I had an interview with him, and he showed a certain want of temper that sent me to bed still irritated. That night I had no dream.

Nor did I dream the next night, at least, to remember.

"Something of that intense reality of conviction vanished. I began to feel sure it was a dream. And then it came again.

"When the dream came again, nearly four days later, it was very different. I think it certain that four days had also elapsed in the dream. Many things had happened in the north, and the shadow of them was back again between us, and this time it was not so easily dispelled. I began I know with moody musings. Why, in spite of all, should I go back, go back for all the rest of my days to toil and stress, insults and perpetual dissatisfaction, simply to save hundreds of millions of common people, whom I did not love, whom too often I could do no other than despise, from the stress and anguish of war and infinite misrule? And after all I might fail. They all sought their own narrow ends, and why should not I—why should not I also live as a man? And out of such thoughts her voice summoned me, and I lifted my eyes.

"I found myself awake and walking. We had come out above the Pleasure City, we were near the summit of Monte Solaro and looking towards the bay. It was the late afternoon and very clear. Far away to the left Ischia hung in a golden haze between sea and sky, and Naples was coldly white against the hills, and before us was Vesuvius with a tall and slender streamer feathering at last towards the south, and the ruins of Torre dell' Annunziata and Castellammare glittering and near."

I interrupted suddenly: "You have been to Capri, of course?"

"Only in this dream," he said, "only in this dream. All across the bay beyond Sorrento were the floating palaces of the Pleasure City moored and chained. And northward were the broad floating stages that received the aeroplanes. Aeroplanes fell out of the sky every afternoon, each bringing its thousands of pleasure-seekers from the uttermost parts of the earth to Capri and its delights. All these things, I say, stretched below.

"But we noticed them only incidentally because of an unusual sight that evening had to show. Five war aeroplanes that had long slumbered useless in the distant arsenals of the Rhinemouth were manoeuvring now in the eastward sky. Evesham had astonished the world by producing them and others, and sending them to circle here and there. It was the threat material in the great game of bluff he was playing, and it had taken even me by surprise. He was one of those incredibly stupid energetic people who seem sent by heaven to create disasters. His energy to the first glance seemed so wonderfully like capacity! But he had no imagination, no invention, only a stupid, vast, driving force of will, and a mad faith in his stupid idiot 'luck' to pull him through. I remember how we stood upon the headland watching the squadron circling far away, and how I weighed the full meaning of the sight, seeing clearly the way things must go. And then even it was not too late. I might have gone back, I think, and saved the world. The people of the north would follow me, I knew, granted only that in one thing I respected their moral standards. The east and south would trust me as they would trust no other northern man. And I knew I had only to put it to her and she would have let me go . . . . Not because she did not love me!

"Only I did not want to go; my will was all the other way about. I had so newly thrown off the incubus of responsibility: I was still so fresh a renegade from duty that the daylight clearness of what I ought to do had no power at all to touch my will. My will was to live, to gather pleasures and make my dear lady happy. But though this sense of vast neglected duties had no power to draw me, it could make me silent and preoccupied, it robbed the days I had spent of half their brightness and roused me into dark meditations in the silence of the night. And as I stood and watched Evesham's aeroplanes sweep to and fro—those birds of infinite ill omen—she stood beside me watching me, perceiving the trouble indeed, but not perceiving it clearly—her eyes questioning my face, her expression shaded with perplexity. Her face was gray because the sunset was fading out of the sky. It was no fault of hers that she held me. She had asked me to go from her, and again in the night time and with tears she had asked me to go.

"At last it was the sense of her that roused me from my mood.

I turned upon her suddenly and challenged her to race down the mountain slopes. 'No,' she said, as if I had jarred with her gravity, but I was resolved to end that gravity, and make her run—no one can be very gray and sad who is out of breath—and when she stumbled I ran with my hand beneath her arm. We ran down past a couple of men, who turned back staring in astonishment at my behaviour—they must have recognised my face. And half way down the slope came a tumult in the air, clang-clank, clang-clank, and we stopped, and presently over the hill-crest those war things came flying one behind the other."

The man seemed hesitating on the verge of a description.

"What were they like?" I asked.

"They had never fought," he said. "They were just like our ironclads are nowadays; they had never fought. No one knew what they might do, with excited men inside them; few even cared to speculate. They were great driving things shaped like spear-heads without a shaft, with a propeller in the place of the shaft."

"Steel?"

"Not steel."

"Aluminum?"

"No, no, nothing of that sort. An alloy that was very common—as common as brass, for example. It was called—let me see—" He squeezed his forehead with the fingers of one hand. "I am forgetting everything," he said.

"And they carried guns?"

"Little guns, firing high explosive shells. They fired the guns backwards, out of the base of the leaf, so to speak, and rammed with the beak. That was the theory, you know, but they had never been fought. No one could tell exactly what was going to happen. And meanwhile I suppose it was very fine to go whirling through the air like a flight of young swallows, swift and easy. I guess the captains tried not to think too clearly what the real thing would be like. And these flying war machines, you know, were only one sort of the endless war contrivances that had been invented and had fallen into abeyance during the long peace. There were all sorts of these things that people were routing out and furbishing up; infernal things, silly things; things that had never been tried; big engines, terrible explosives, great guns. You know the silly way of these ingenious sort of men who make these things; they turn 'em out as beavers build dams, and with no more sense of the rivers they're going to divert and the lands they're going to flood!

"As we went down the winding stepway to our hotel again, in the twilight, I foresaw it all: I saw how clearly and inevitably things were driving for war in Evesham's silly, violent hands, and I had some inkling of what war was bound to be under these new conditions. And even then, though I knew it was drawing near the limit of my opportunity, I could find no will to go back."

He sighed.

"That was my last chance.

"We didn't go into the city until the sky was full of stars, so we walked out upon the high terrace, to and fro, and—she counselled me to go back.

"'My dearest,' she said, and her sweet face looked up to me, 'this is Death. This life you lead is Death. Go back to them, go back to your duty—'

"She began to weep, saying, between her sobs, and clinging to my arm as she said it, 'Go back—Go back.'

"Then suddenly she fell mute, and, glancing down at her face, I read in an instant the thing she had thought to do. It was one of those moments when one sees.

"'No!' I said.

"'No?' she asked, in surprise and I think a little fearful at the answer to her thought.

"'Nothing,' I said, 'shall send me back. Nothing! I have chosen. Love, I have chosen, and the world must go. Whatever happens I will live this life—I will live for you! It—nothing shall turn me aside; nothing, my dear one. Even if you died—even if you died—'

"'Yes?' she murmured, softly.

"'Then—I also would die.'

"And before she could speak again I began to talk, talking eloquently—as I could do in that life—talking to exalt love, to make the life we were living seem heroic and glorious; and the thing I was deserting something hard and enormously ignoble that it was a fine thing to set aside. I bent all my mind to throw that glamour upon it, seeking not only to convert her but myself to that. We talked, and she clung to me, torn too between all that she deemed noble and all that she knew was sweet. And at last I did make it heroic, made all the thickening disaster of the world only a sort of glorious setting to our unparalleled love, and we two poor foolish souls strutted there at last, clad in that splendid delusion, drunken rather with that glorious delusion, under the still stars.

"And so my moment passed.

"It was my last chance. Even as we went to and fro there, the leaders of the south and east were gathering their resolve, and the hot answer that shattered Evesham's bluffing for ever, took shape and waited. And, all over Asia, and the ocean, and the South, the air and the wires were throbbing with their warnings to prepare—prepare.

"No one living, you know, knew what war was; no one could imagine, with all these new inventions, what horror war might bring. I believe most people still believed it would be a matter of bright uniforms and shouting charges and triumphs and flags and bands—in a time when half the world drew its food supply from regions ten thousand miles away—"

The man with the white face paused. I glanced at him, and his face was intent on the floor of the carriage. A little railway station, a string of loaded trucks, a signal-box, and the back of a cottage, shot by the carriage window, and a bridge passed with a clap of noise, echoing the tumult of the train.

"After that," he said, "I dreamt often. For three weeks of nights that dream was my life. And the worst of it was there were nights when I could not dream, when I lay tossing on a bed in this accursed life; and there—somewhere lost to me—things were happening—momentous, terrible things . . . I lived at nights—my days, my waking days, this life I am living now, became a faded, far-away dream, a drab setting, the cover of the book."

He thought.

"I could tell you all, tell you every little thing in the dream, but as to what I did in the daytime—no. I could not tell—I do not remember. My memory—my memory has gone. The business of life slips from me—"

He leant forward, and pressed his hands upon his eyes. For a long time he said nothing.

"And then?" said I.

"The war burst like a hurricane."

He stared before him at unspeakable things.

"And then?" I urged again.

"One touch of unreality," he said, in the low tone of a man who speaks to himself, "and they would have been nightmares. But they were not nightmares—they were not nightmares. No!"

He was silent for so long that it dawned upon me that there was a danger of losing the rest of the story. But he went on talking again in the same tone of questioning self-communion.

"What was there to do but flight? I had not thought the war would touch Capri—I had seemed to see Capri as being out of it all, as the contrast to it all; but two nights after the whole place was shouting and bawling, every woman almost and every other man wore a badge—Evesham's badge—and there was no music but a jangling war-song over and over again, and everywhere men enlisting, and in the dancing halls they were drilling. The whole island was awhirl with rumours; it was said, again and again, that fighting had begun. I had not expected this. I had seen so little of the life of pleasure that I had failed to reckon with this violence of the amateurs. And as for me, I was out of it. I was like the man who might have prevented the firing of a magazine. The time had gone. I was no one; the vainest stripling with a badge counted for more than I. The crowd jostled us and bawled in our ears; that accursed song deafened us; a woman shrieked at my lady because no badge was on her, and we two went back to our own place again, ruffled and insulted—my lady white and silent, and I aquiver with rage. So furious was I, I could have quarrelled with her if I could have found one shade of accusation in her eyes.

"All my magnificence had gone from me. I walked up and down our rock cell, and outside was the darkling sea and a light to the southward that flared and passed and came again.

"'We must get out of this place,' I said over and over. 'I have made my choice, and I will have no hand in these troubles. I will have nothing of this war. We have taken our lives out of all these things. This is no refuge for us. Let us go.'

"And the next day we were already in flight from the war that covered the world.

"And all the rest was Flight—all the rest was Flight."

He mused darkly.

"How much was there of it?"

He made no answer.

"How many days?"

His face was white and drawn and his hands were clenched. He took no heed of my curiosity.

I tried to draw him back to his story with questions.

"Where did you go?" I said.

"When?"

"When you left Capri."

"South-west," he said, and glanced at me for a second. "We went in a boat."

"But I should have thought an aeroplane?"

"They had been seized."

I questioned him no more. Presently I thought he was beginning again. He broke out in an argumentative monotone:

"But why should it be? If, indeed, this battle, this slaughter and stress is life, why have we this craving for pleasure and beauty? If there is no refuge, if there is no place of peace, and if all our dreams of quiet places are a folly and a snare, why have we such dreams? Surely it was no ignoble cravings, no base intentions, had brought us to this; it was Love had isolated us. Love had come to me with her eyes and robed in her beauty, more glorious than all else in life, in the very shape and colour of life, and summoned me away. I had silenced all the voices, I had answered all the questions—I had come to her. And suddenly there was nothing but War and Death!"

I had an inspiration. "After all," I said, "it could have been only a dream."

"A dream!" he cried, flaming upon me, "a dream—when, even now—"

For the first time he became animated. A faint flush crept into his cheek. He raised his open hand and clenched it, and dropped it to his knee. He spoke, looking away from me, and for all the rest of the time he looked away. "We are but phantoms!" he said, "and the phantoms of phantoms, desires like cloud-shadows and wills of straw that eddy in the wind; the days pass, use and wont carry us through as a train carries the shadow of its lights—so be it! But one thing is real and certain, one thing is no dream-stuff, but eternal and enduring. It is the centre of my life, and all other things about it are subordinate or altogether vain. I loved her, that woman of a dream. And she and I are dead together!

"A dream! How can it be a dream, when it drenched a living life with unappeasable sorrow, when it makes all that I have lived for and cared for, worthless and unmeaning?

"Until that very moment when she was killed I believed we had still a chance of getting away," he said. "All through the night and morning that we sailed across the sea from Capri to Salerno, we talked of escape. We were full of hope, and it clung about us to the end, hope for the life together we should lead, out of it all, out of the battle and struggle, the wild and empty passions, the empty arbitrary 'thou shalt' and 'thou shalt not' of the world. We were uplifted, as though our quest was a holy thing, as though love for another was a mission . . . .

"Even when from our boat we saw the fair face of that great rock Capri—already scarred and gashed by the gun emplacements and hiding-places that were to make it a fastness—we reckoned nothing of the imminent slaughter, though the fury of preparation hung about in the puffs and clouds of dust at a hundred points amidst the gray; but, indeed, I made a text of that and talked. There, you know, was the rock, still beautiful for all its scars, with its countless windows and arches and ways, tier upon tier, for a thousand feet, a vast carving of gray, broken by vine-clad terraces, and lemon and orange groves, and masses of agave and prickly pear, and puffs of almond blossom. And out under the archway that is built over the Piccola Marina other boats were coming; and as we came round the cape and within sight of the mainland, another little string of boats came into view, driving before the wind towards the south-west. In a little while a multitude had come out, the remoter just little specks of ultramarine in the shadow of the eastward cliff.

"'It is love and reason,' I said, 'fleeing from all this madness of war.'

"And though we presently saw a squadron of aeroplanes flying across the southern sky we did not heed it. There it was—a line of little dots in the sky—and then more, dotting the south-eastern horizon, and then still more, until all that quarter of the sky was stippled with blue specks. Now they were all thin little strokes of blue, and now one and now a multitude would heel and catch the sun and become short flashes of light. They came, rising and falling and growing larger, like some huge flight of gulls or rooks or such-like birds, moving with a marvellous uniformity, and ever as they drew nearer they spread over a greater width of sky. The southward wind flung itself in an arrow-headed cloud athwart the sun. And then suddenly they swept round to the eastward and streamed eastward, growing smaller and smaller and clearer and clearer again until they vanished from the sky. And after that we noted to the northward and very high Evesham's fighting machines hanging high over Naples like an evening swarm of gnats.

"It seemed to have no more to do with us than a flight of birds.

"Even the mutter of guns far away in the south-east seemed to us to signify nothing . . .

"Each day, each dream after that, we were still exalted, still seeking that refuge where we might live and love. Fatigue had come upon us, pain and many distresses. For though we were dusty and stained by our toilsome tramping, and half starved and with the horror of the dead men we had seen and the flight of the peasants—for very soon a gust of fighting swept up the peninsula—with these things haunting our minds it still resulted only in a deepening resolution to escape. Oh, but she was brave and patient! She who had never faced hardship and exposure had courage for herself and me. We went to and fro seeking an outlet, over a country all commandeered and ransacked by the gathering hosts of war. Always we went on foot. At first there were other fugitives, but we did not mingle with them. Some escaped northward, some were caught in the torrent of peasantry that swept along the main roads; many gave themselves into the hands of the soldiery and were sent northward. Many of the men were impressed. But we kept away from these things; we had brought no money to bribe a passage north, and I feared for my lady at the hands of these conscript crowds. We had landed at Salerno, and we had been turned back from Cava, and we had tried to cross towards Taranto by a pass over Mount Alburno, but we had been driven back for want of food, and so we had come down among the marshes by Paestum, where those great temples stand alone. I had some vague idea that by Paestum it might be possible to find a boat or something, and take once more to sea. And there it was the battle overtook us.

"A sort of soul-blindness had me. Plainly I could see that we were being hemmed in; that the great net of that giant Warfare had us in its toils. Many times we had seen the levies that had come down from the north going to and fro, and had come upon them in the distance amidst the mountains making ways for the ammunition and preparing the mounting of the guns. Once we fancied they had fired at us, taking us for spies—at any rate a shot had gone shuddering over us. Several times we had hidden in woods from hovering aeroplanes.

"But all these things do not matter now, these nights of flight and pain . . . We were in an open place near those great temples at Paestum, at last, on a blank stony place dotted with spiky bushes, empty and desolate and so flat that a grove of eucalyptus far away showed to the feet of its stems. How I can see it! My lady was sitting down under a bush resting a little, for she was very weak and weary, and I was standing up watching to see if I could tell the distance of the firing that came and went. They were still, you know, fighting far from each other, with those terrible new weapons that had never before been used: guns that would carry beyond sight, and aeroplanes that would do—What they would do no man could foretell.

"I knew that we were between the two armies, and that they drew together. I knew we were in danger, and that we could not stop there and rest!

"Though all these things were in my mind, they were in the background. They seemed to be affairs beyond our concern. Chiefly, I was thinking of my lady. An aching distress filled me. For the first time she had owned herself beaten and had fallen a-weeping. Behind me I could hear her sobbing, but I would not turn round to her because I knew she had need of weeping, and had held herself so far and so long for me. It was well, I thought, that she would weep and rest and then we would toil on again, for I had no inkling of the thing that hung so near. Even now I can see her as she sat there, her lovely hair upon her shoulder, can mark again the deepening hollow of her cheek.

"'If we had parted,' she said, 'if I had let you go.'

"'No,' said I.' Even now, I do not repent. I will not repent;
I made my choice, and I will hold on to the end.'
"And then—

"Overhead in the sky flashed something and burst, and all about us I heard the bullets making a noise like a handful of peas suddenly thrown. They chipped the stones about us, and whirled fragments from the bricks and passed . . . ."

He put his hand to his mouth, and then moistened his lips.

"At the flash I had turned about . . .

"You know—she stood up—

"She stood up, you know, and moved a step towards me—as though she wanted to reach me—

"And she had been shot through the heart."

He stopped and stared at me. I felt all that foolish incapacity an Englishman feels on such occasions. I met his eyes for a moment, and then stared out of the window. For a long space we kept silence. When at last I looked at him he was sitting back in his corner, his arms folded, and his teeth gnawing at his knuckles.

He bit his nail suddenly, and stared at it.

"I carried her," he said, "towards the temples, in my arms—as though it mattered. I don't know why. They seemed a sort of sanctuary, you know, they had lasted so long, I suppose.

"She must have died almost instantly. Only—I talked to her all the way."

Silence again.

"I have seen those temples," I said abruptly, and indeed he had brought those still, sunlit arcades of worn sandstone very vividly before me.

"It was the brown one, the big brown one. I sat down on a fallen pillar and held her in my arms . . . Silent after the first babble was over. And after a little while the lizards came out and ran about again, as though nothing unusual was going on, as though nothing had changed . . . It was tremendously still there, the sun high and the shadows still; even the shadows of the weeds upon the entablature were still—in spite of the thudding and banging that went all about the sky.

"I seem to remember that the aeroplanes came up out of the south, and that the battle went away to the west. One aeroplane was struck, and overset and fell. I remember that—though it didn't interest me in the least. It didn't seem to signify. It was like a wounded gull, you know—flapping for a time in the water. I could see it down the aisle of the temple—a black thing in the bright blue water.

"Three or four times shells burst about the beach, and then that ceased. Each time that happened all the lizards scuttled in and hid for a space. That was all the mischief done, except that once a stray bullet gashed the stone hard by—made just a fresh bright surface.

"As the shadows grew longer, the stillness seemed greater.

"The curious thing," he remarked, with the manner of a man who makes a trivial conversation, "is that I didn't think—at all. I sat with her in my arms amidst the stones—in a sort of lethargy—stagnant.

"And I don't remember waking up. I don't remember dressing that day. I know I found myself in my office, with my letters all slit open in front of me, and how I was struck by the absurdity of being there, seeing that in reality I was sitting, stunned, in that Paestum Temple with a dead woman in my arms. I read my letters like a machine. I have forgotten what they were about."

He stopped, and there was a long silence.

Suddenly I perceived that we were running down the incline from Chalk Farm to Euston. I started at this passing of time. I turned on him with a brutal question, with the tone of "Now or never."

"And did you dream again?"

"Yes."

He seemed to force himself to finish. His voice was very low.

"Once more, and as it were only for a few instants. I seemed to have suddenly awakened out of a great apathy, to have risen into a sitting position, and the body lay there on the stones beside me. A gaunt body. Not her, you know. So soon—it was not her . . . .

"I may have heard voices. I do not know. Only I knew clearly that men were coming into the solitude and that that was a last outrage.

"I stood up and walked through the temple, and then there came into sight—first one man with a yellow face, dressed in a uniform of dirty white, trimmed with blue, and then several, climbing to the crest of the old wall of the vanished city, and crouching there. They were little bright figures in the sunlight, and there they hung, weapon in hand, peering cautiously before them.

"And further away I saw others and then more at another point in the wall. It was a long lax line of men in open order.

"Presently the man I had first seen stood up and shouted a command, and his men came tumbling down the wall and into the high weeds towards the temple. He scrambled down with them and led them. He came facing towards me, and when he saw me he stopped.

"At first I had watched these men with a mere curiosity, but when I had seen they meant to come to the temple I was moved to forbid them. I shouted to the officer.

"'You must not come here,' I cried, 'I am here. I am here with my dead.'

"He stared, and then shouted a question back to me in some unknown tongue.

"I repeated what I had said.

"He shouted again, and I folded my arms and stood still. Presently he spoke to his men and came forward. He carried a drawn sword.

"I signed to him to keep away, but he continued to advance. I told him again very patiently and clearly: 'You must not come here. These are old temples and I am here with my dead.'

"Presently he was so close I could see his face clearly. It was a narrow face, with dull gray eyes, and a black moustache. He had a scar on his upper lip, and he was dirty and unshaven. He kept shouting unintelligible things, questions, perhaps, at me.

"I know now that he was afraid of me, but at the time that did not occur to me. As I tried to explain to him, he interrupted me in imperious tones, bidding me, I suppose, stand aside.

"He made to go past me, and I caught hold of him.

"I saw his face change at my grip.

"'You fool,' I cried. 'Don't you know? She is dead!'

"He started back. He looked at me with cruel eyes. I saw a sort of exultant resolve leap into them—delight. Then, suddenly, with a scowl, he swept his sword back—so—and thrust."

He stopped abruptly.

I became aware of a change in the rhythm of the train. The brakes lifted their voices and the carriage jarred and jerked. This present world insisted upon itself, became clamourous. I saw through the steamy window huge electric fights glaring down from tall masts upon a fog, saw rows of stationary empty carriages passing by, and then a signal-box hoisting its constellation of green and red into the murky London twilight, marched after them. I looked again at his drawn features.

"He ran me through the heart. It was with a sort of astonishment—no fear, no pain—but just amazement, that I felt it pierce me, felt the sword drive home into my body. It didn't hurt, you know. It didn't hurt at all."

The yellow platform lights came into the field of view, passing first rapidly, then slowly, and at last stopping with a jerk. Dim shapes of men passed to and fro without.

"Euston!" cried a voice.

"Do you mean—?"

"There was no pain, no sting or smart. Amazement and then darkness sweeping over everything. The hot, brutal face before me, the face of the man who had killed me, seemed to recede. It swept out of existence—"

"Euston!" clamoured the voices outside; "Euston!"

The carriage door opened admitting a flood of sound, and a porter stood regarding us. The sounds of doors slamming, and the hoof-clatter of cab-horses, and behind these things the featureless remote roar of the London cobble-stones, came to my ears. A truckload of lighted lamps blazed along the platform.

"A darkness, a flood of darkness that opened and spread and blotted out all things."

"Any luggage, sir?" said the porter.

"And that was the end?" I asked.

He seemed to hesitate. Then, almost inaudibly, he answered, "no."

"You mean?"

"I couldn't get to her. She was there on the other side of the temple— And then—"

"Yes," I insisted. "Yes?"

"Nightmares," he cried; "nightmares indeed! My God! Great

birds that fought and tore."

www.ingramcontent.com/pod-product-compliance
Lightning Source LLC
LaVergne TN
LVHW051023080826
845145LV00009B/2767

* 9 7 8 1 7 8 7 2 4 5 8 0 8 *